# THE ZOMBIE NITE CAFÉ

by Merrily Kutner

illustrated by Ethan Long

Holiday House / New York

Library of Congress Cataloging-in-Publication Data
Kutner, Merrily.
The Zombie Nite Café / by Merrily Kutner; illustrated by Ethan Long.– 1st ed.
p. cm.
Summary: While walking the dog late one evening, a young child stumbles
across the spooky Zombie Nite Café and describes the scary creatures dining inside.
ISBN-10: 0-8234-1963-0 (hardcover)
ISBN-13: 978-0-8234-1963-0
[1. Zombies–Fiction. 2. Monsters–Fiction.
3. Stories in rhyme.]
I. Long, Ethan, ill. II. Title.
PZ8.3.K965 Zom 2007
[E]–dc22
2005050333

For my husband, Bruce,
A monster in his own right!
M. K.

For Rob, Dom, and Paulo,
and all those late nights
E. L.

Through the fog at half past nine,
I saw the flashing neon sign.
A stranger place I'd never seen,
With monsters–was it Halloween?
While out to walk my dog, JJ,
I found the Zombie Nite Café.

The Ghouls and Trolls were out that night
With more than just an appetite.
The dead and undead came to meet,
They shuffled in right off the street.
And heavy smells of foul decay
Seeped through the Zombie Nite Café.

YOUR
HOSTESS
WILL
SEAT
YOU

A veiny Eyeball slithered in,
Followed by a Hobgoblin.
Aliens beamed down from their ship
To grab some grub before their trip,
Their course set for the Milky Way
Beyond the Zombie Nite Café.

A Werewolf crept upon all fours,
It shattered the glass entry doors.
Frankenstein's Monster and his Bride
Spotted a booth and lurched inside.
They didn't have a lot to say
In the Zombie Nite Café.

Bigfoot loomed over ten feet tall,
Crashed through the booth to make a call.
The Bogeyman had just dropped by
And met his friend with one huge eye
To celebrate one more birthday
In the Zombie Nite Café.

The Headless Horseman gripped his head,
While from his coat dripped something red.
With flaming pumpkin by his side,
He had a snack before his ride,
Then made his speedy getaway
From the Zombie Night Café.

The owner rose up from the floor,
Then vanished through a secret door.
Another Zombie left his tomb
And staggered right across the room
To feast upon the dread buffet
In the Zombie Nite Café.

Through the window Dracula flew,
He ordered something reddish blue.
Hovering Specters caught my eyes,
They'd come to drink and socialize.
The spirits laughed; I heard them say,
"You'll never leave Zombie Café!"

She said I'd better order soon.
"Today's special," I heard her say,
"Is Eyes Flambé Zombie Café."

I checked the menu one more time,
Then ordered number three—no slime.
"We don't serve scrambled brains to go. . . .
They're better hot, don't cha know?
Take number eight, if that's okay,
All's fresh in Zombie Nite Café!"

PLEASE USE # WHEN ORDERING
1. CHICKEN MCMAGGOTS
2. FLESH WOUND ON WHEAT
3. SCRAMBLED BRAINS
4. AORTA OVER EASY
5. GREEN BEEF STEW
6. TYPE "O" BLOOD PUDDING
7. SCARY SALAD W/ CROUTONS
MALFORMED MEAT PATTY
9. SLOPPER JUNIOR

Then through the swinging kitchen door
Burst a being as none before.
A formless creature neath a hat—
Invisible Cook . . . look at that!
Too late to plan my getaway
From the Zombie Nite Café.

He lunged at me and waved his knife.
This was the battle of my life!
But my JJ was very brave–
He'd save me from an early grave.
His growling kept the cook at bay
As I escaped Zombie Café.

Then JJ howled; to my despair
A force propelled him through the air.
Stuck in his mouth to my surprise
Was some thing's head with beady eyes.
I yanked it out, we sped away
From that Zombie Nite Café.

Off in the woods, no time to roam,
We swiftly found our way back home.
I didn't talk about that night
'Cause who'd believe me . . . no one, right?

But that's the truth–no more to say.
Beware the Zombie Nite Café!